WITHDRAWN

This book belongs to

The 60TH Anniversary Edition

THE LITTLE ENGINE THAT COULD®

Retold by

WATTY PIPER

Illustrated by George & Doris Hauman

NEW YORK
PLATT & MUNK
Publishers

GROSSET & DUNLAP
Published by the Penguin Group
Penguin Group (USA) Inc., 375 Hudson Street, New York, New York 10014, USA
Penguin Group (Canada), 90 Eglinton Avenue East, Suite 700, Toronto, Ontario M4P 2Y3, Canada
(a division of Pearson Penguin Canada Inc.)
Penguin Books Ltd, 80 Strand, London WC2R 0RL, England
Penguin Ireland, 25 St Stephen's Green, Dublin 2, Ireland (a division of Penguin Books Ltd)
Penguin Group (Australia), 707 Collins Street, Melbourne, Victoria 3008, Australia
(a division of Pearson Australia Group Pty Ltd)
Penguin Books India Pvt Ltd, 11 Community Centre, Panchsheel Park, New Delhi—110 017, India
Penguin Group (NZ), 67 Apollo Drive, Rosedale, Auckland 0632, New Zealand
(a division of Pearson New Zealand Ltd)
Penguin Books (South Africa), Rosebank Office Park, 181 Jan Smuts Avenue, Parktown North 2193, South Africa
Penguin China, B7 Jiaming Center, 27 East Third Ring Road North, Chaoyang District, Beijing 100020, China

Penguin Books Ltd, Registered Offices: 80 Strand, London WC2R 0RL, England

Copyright © 1976, 1961, 1951, 1945, 1930 by Penguin Group (USA) Inc. All rights reserved. The Little Engine That Could®, I Think I Can®, and all related titles, logos, and characters are trademarks of Penguin Group (USA) Inc. Published by Platt & Munk, Publishers, an imprint of Grosset & Dunlap, a division of Penguin Young Readers Group, 345 Hudson Street, New York, New York 10014. Printed in the U.S.A.

60th Anniversary Edition published in 1990
by Platt & Munk, Publishers, New York.

Library of Congress Catalog Card Number: 89-81287

ISBN 978-0-448-40041-9   41 40 39

Chug, chug, chug. Puff, puff, puff. Ding-dong, ding-dong. The little train rumbled over the tracks.

She was a happy little train for she had such a jolly load to carry. Her cars were filled full of good things for boys and girls.

There were toy animals—giraffes with long necks, Teddy bears with almost no necks at all, and even a baby elephant.

Then there were dolls—dolls with blue eyes and yellow curls, dolls with brown eyes and brown bobbed heads, and the funniest little toy clown you ever saw.

And there were cars full of toy engines, airplanes, tops, jack-knives, picture puzzles, books, and every kind of thing boys or girls could want.

But that was not all. Some of the cars were filled with all sorts
of good things for boys and girls to eat—big golden oranges,
red-cheeked apples, bottles of creamy milk for their breakfasts,

fresh spinach for their dinners, peppermint drops, and lollypops for after-meal treats.

The little train was carrying all these wonderful things to the
good little boys and girls on the other side of the mountain.

She puffed along merrily. Then all of a sudden she stopped with a jerk. She simply could not go another inch. She tried and she tried, but her wheels would not turn.

What were all those good little boys and girls on the other side of the mountain going to do without the wonderful toys to play with and the good food to eat?

"Here comes a shiny new engine," said the funny little clown who jumped out of the train.

"Let us ask him to help us."

So all the dolls and toys cried out together, "Please, Shiny New Engine, won't you please pull our train over the mountain? Our engine has broken down, and the boys and girls on the other side won't have any toys to play with or good food to eat unless you help us."

But the Shiny New Engine snorted: "I pull you? I am a Passenger Engine. I have just carried a fine big train over the mountain, with more cars than you ever dreamed of. My train had sleeping cars, with comfortable berths; a dining car where waiters bring whatever hungry people want to eat; and parlor cars in which people sit in soft armchairs and look out of big plate-glass windows. I pull the likes of you? Indeed not!"

And off he steamed to the roundhouse, where engines live when they are not busy. How sad the little train and all the dolls and toys felt!

Then the little clown called out, "The Passenger Engine is not the only one in the world. Here is another engine coming, a great big strong one. Let us ask him to help us."

The little toy clown waved his flag and the big strong engine came to a stop.

"Please, oh, please, Big Engine," cried all the dolls and toys together. "Won't you please pull our train over the mountain?

Our engine has broken down, and the good little boys and girls on the other side won't have any toys to play with or good food to eat unless you help us."

But the Big Strong Engine bellowed: "I am a Freight Engine. I have just pulled a big train loaded with big machines over the mountain. These machines print books and newspapers for grown-ups to read. I am a very important engine indeed. I won't pull the likes of you!" And the Freight Engine puffed off indignantly to the roundhouse.

The little train and all the dolls and toys were very sad.

"Cheer up," cried the little toy clown. "The Freight Engine is not the only one in the world. Here comes another. He looks very old and tired, but our train is so little, perhaps he can help us."

So the little toy clown waved his flag and the dingy, rusty old engine stopped.

"Please, Kind Engine," cried all the dolls and toys together. "Won't you please pull our train over the mountain? Our engine has broken down, and the boys and girls on the other side won't have any toys to play with or good food to eat unless you help us."

But the Rusty Old Engine sighed, "I am so tired. I must rest my weary wheels. I cannot pull even so little a train as yours over the mountain. I can not. I can not. I can not."

And off he rumbled to the roundhouse chugging, "I can not. I can not. I can not."

Then indeed the little train was very, very sad, and the dolls and toys were ready to cry.

But the little clown called out, "Here is another engine coming, a little blue engine, a very little one, maybe she will help us."

The very little engine came chug, chugging merrily along. When she saw the toy clown's flag, she stopped quickly.

"What is the matter, my friends?" she asked kindly.

"Oh, Little Blue Engine," cried the dolls and toys. "Will you pull us over the mountain? Our engine has broken down and the good boys and girls on the other side won't have any toys to play with or good food to eat, unless you help us. Please, please help us, Little Blue Engine."

"I'm not very big," said the Little Blue Engine. "They use me only for switching trains in the yard. I have never been over the mountain."

"But we must get over the mountain before the children

awake," said all the dolls and the toys.

The very little engine looked up and saw the tears in the dolls' eyes. And she thought of the good little boys and girls on the other side of the mountain who would not have any toys or good food unless she helped.

Then she said, "I think I can. I think I can. I think I can." And she hitched herself to the little train.

She tugged and pulled and pulled and tugged and slowly, slowly, slowly they started off.

The toy clown jumped aboard and all the dolls and the toy animals began to smile and cheer.

Puff, puff, chug, chug, went the Little Blue Engine. "I think I can—I think I can—I think I can—I think I can—I think I can—I think I can—I think I can—I think I can—I think I can."

Up, up, up. Faster and faster and faster the little engine climbed, until at last they reached the top of the mountain.

Down in the valley lay the city.

"Hurray, hurray," cried the funny little clown and all the dolls and toys. "The good little boys and girls in the city will be happy because you helped us, kind Little Blue Engine."

And the Little Blue Engine smiled and seemed to say as she puffed steadily down the mountain…

"I thought I could. I thought I could. I thought I could.
I thought I could.

I thought I could.

I thought I could."

The kindness and determination of the Little Blue Engine have inspired millions of children around the world since the story was first published in 1930. Cherished by readers for sixty years, *The Little Engine That Could* is a classic of childhood. This special anniversary edition contains the complete and original text and artwork.